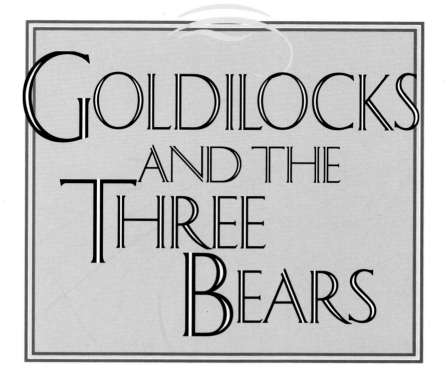

GOLDILOCKS AND THE THREE BEARS

TOLD IN SIGNED ENGLISH

Harry Bornstein
Karen Luczak Saulnier

Illustrated by Annie Lunsford

Sign drawings by Jan Skrobisz

Kendall Green Publications
Gallaudet University Press
Washington, D.C.

KENDALL GREEN PUBLICATIONS
An imprint of Gallaudet University Press
800 Florida Avenue NE
Washington, DC 20002

Printed in Hong Kong

Book design by Sharon Davis Thorpe, Panache Designs

Library of Congress Cataloging-in-Publication Data

Bornstein, Harry
    Goldilocks and the three bears told in Signed English / Harry Bornstein, Karen Luczak Saulnier : illustrated
by Annie Lunsford : sign drawings by Jan Skrobisz.
      p. cm.
    Summary: The well-known tale about the little girl who wanders through the woods and disturbs the house
of the three bears, accompanied by diagrams showing how to form the Signed English signs for each word of the text.
    ISBN 1-56368-057-2 (alk. paper)
    1. Sign language--Juvenile literature. [1. Folklore. 2. Bears--Folklore. 3. Sign Language.]
I. Saulnier, Karen Luczak. II. Lunsford, Annie, ill. III. Skrobisz, Jan, ill. IV. Title.
PZ10.4.B65Go 1996
398.24'52974446--dc20
        96-20023
        CIP
        AC

To Parents and Teachers

Goldilocks and the Three Bears is a folktale known and loved by children throughout the world. This book makes the story available to deaf, hard-of-hearing, and language-delayed children in a new and inviting way.

Read the story aloud to your child. Learn the signs so that you can read and sign the story at the same time. This will help your child associate specific signs with specific English words and lip movements. Encourage your child to repeat the signs and words and to retell the story.

Signed English is a communication system that allows its users to simultaneously say and sign the patterns of spoken English. Its manual component is based on American Sign Language but includes invented signs and grammatical sign markers. When properly used, Signed English provides an English-language environment in which deaf, hard-of-hearing, and language-delayed children can learn the vocabulary and structure of English. In Signed English, each sign corresponds to one English word. Words that cannot be represented by signs can be fingerspelled using the American Manual Alphabet.

American Manual Alphabet

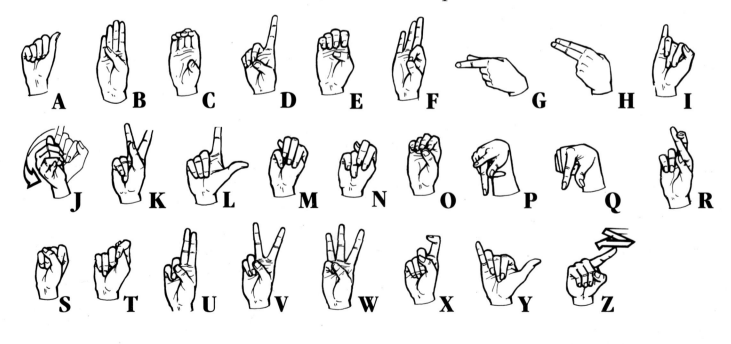

Once	upon	a	time,	there	were

three	bears–	a	great	big	Papa

Bear,	a	middle-	sized	Mama	Bear,

and   a   wee   little   Baby   Bear.

Once upon a time,
there were three bears—
a great big Papa Bear,
a middle-sized Mama Bear,
and a wee little Baby Bear.

They lived in
a house in the woods.
In the living room,
they had three chairs—

They	lived	in	a	house
the	the	woods.	In	the
living	room,	they	had	three	chairs—

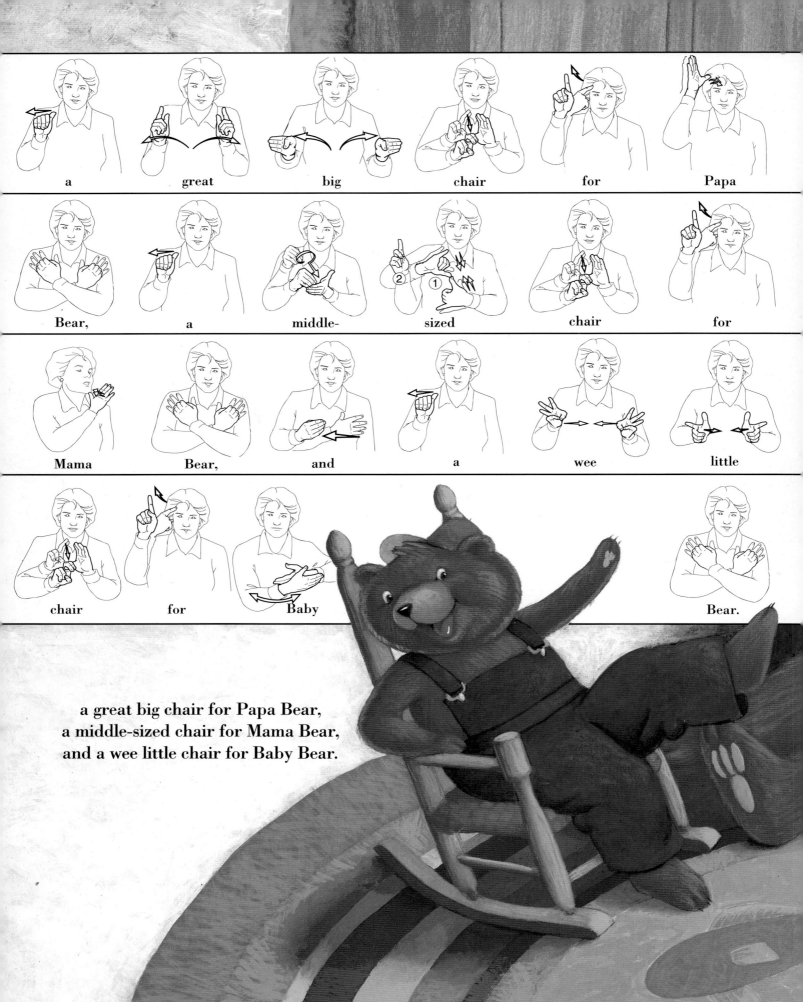

| a | great | big | chair | for | Papa |

| Bear, | a | middle- | sized | chair | for |

| Mama | Bear, | and | a | wee | little |

| chair | for | Baby | | | Bear. |

a great big chair for Papa Bear,
a middle-sized chair for Mama Bear,
and a wee little chair for Baby Bear.

Upstairs, they had three beds —

a great big bed for Papa Bear,
a middle-sized bed for Mama Bear,
and a wee bed for Baby Bear.

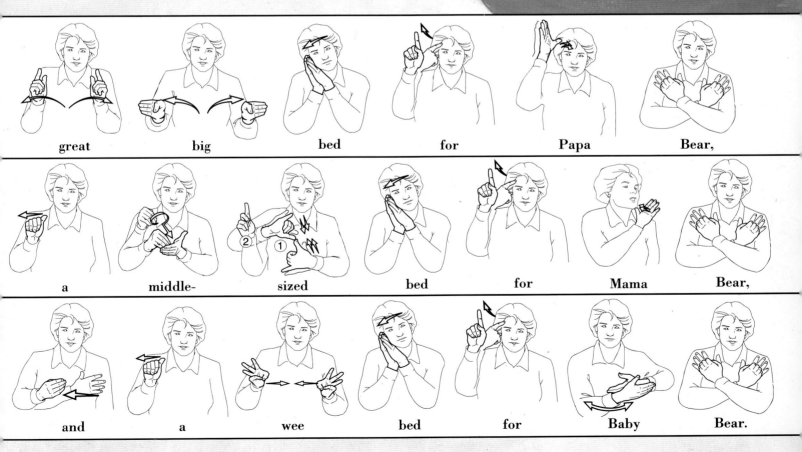

great	big	bed	for	Papa	Bear,
a	middle-	sized	bed	for	Mama	Bear,
and	a	wee	bed	for	Baby	Bear.

One | morning, | Mama | Bear | made | porridge–

a | great | big | bowl | for | Papa

Bear, | a | middle- | sized

One morning, Mama Bear made porridge–
a great big bowl for Papa Bear,
a middle-sized bowl for Mama Bear,
and a wee little bowl for Baby Bear.

bowl   for   Mama   Bear,   and   a

wee   little   bowl   for   Baby   Bear.

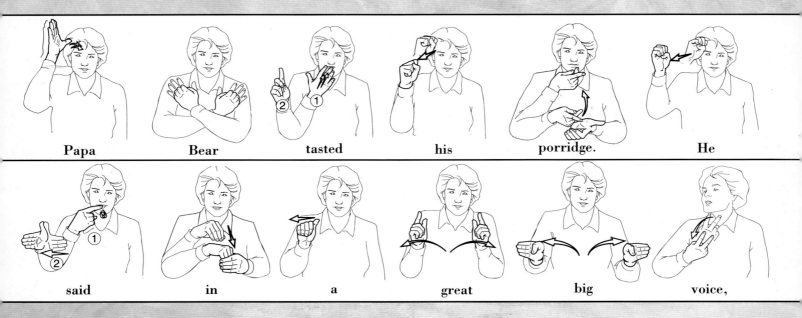

Papa	Bear	tasted	his	porridge.	He

said	in	a	great	big	voice,

Papa Bear tasted his porridge.
He said in a great big voice,
"THIS IS TOO HOT!"
Mama Bear and Baby Bear
tasted their porridge.
It was too hot, too!

THIS   IS   TOO   HOT!   Mama

Bear   and   Baby   Bear   tasted   their

porridge.   It   was   too   hot,   too!

Mama Bear thought for a minute.
She said, "Let's go outside until
our porridge is cool enough to eat."
So the three bears went for
a walk in the woods.

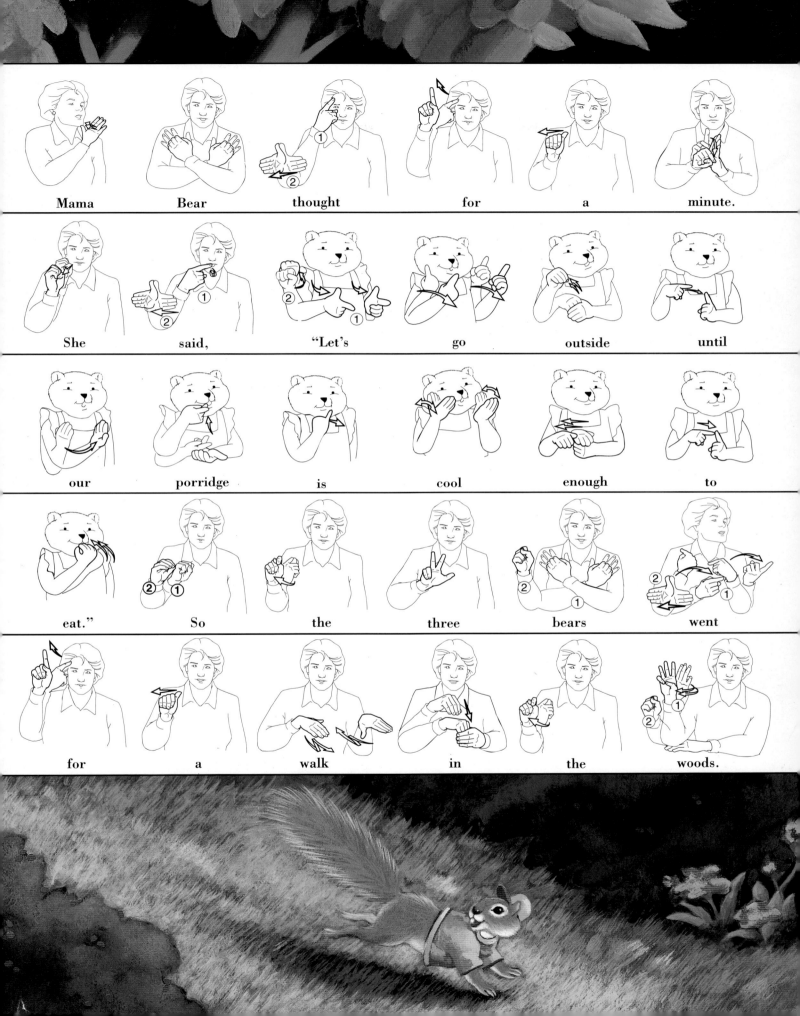

Mama   Bear   thought   for   a   minute.

She   said,   "Let's   go   outside   until

our   porridge   is   cool   enough   to

eat."   So   the   three   bears   went

for   a   walk   in   the   woods.

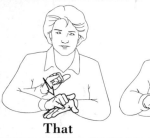 **That** 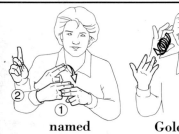 **same** **morning,** **a** **little** **girl**

named **Goldilocks** **was** **skipping** **through** **the**

woods. **She** **saw** **the** **bears'** **house**

and **wondered** **if** **anyone** **was** **home.**

That same morning,
a little girl named Goldilocks
was skipping through the woods.
She saw the bears' house
and wondered if anyone was home.

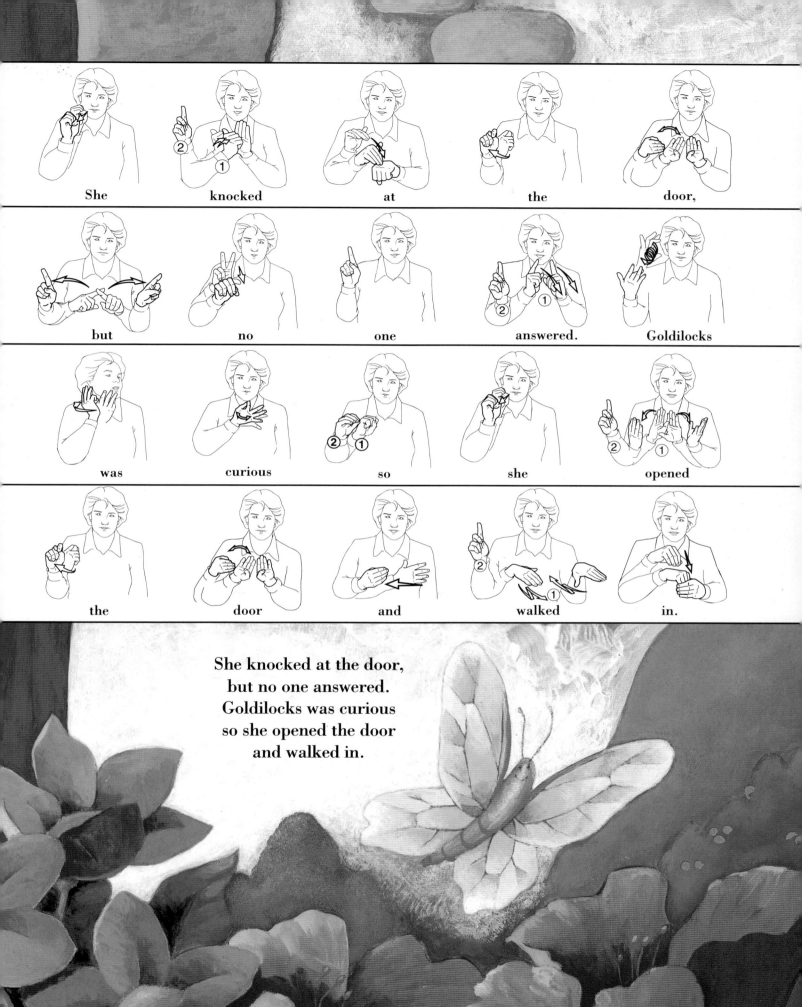

She	knocked	at	the	door,
but	no	one	answered.	Goldilocks
was	curious	so	she	opened
the	door	and	walked	in.

She knocked at the door,
but no one answered.
Goldilocks was curious
so she opened the door
and walked in.

 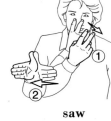   

She saw the porridge on

the table. "Oh, goody," she said,

"I'm hungry." She tasted the porridge

in Papa Bear's bowl, but it

was too hot!

She saw the porridge
on the table. "Oh, goody,"
she said, "I'm hungry."
She tasted the porridge
in Papa Bear's bowl,
but it was too hot!

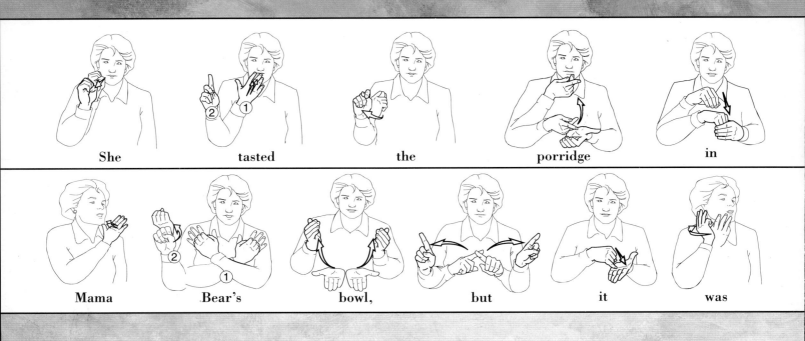

She tasted the porridge
in Mama Bear's bowl,
but it was too cold!
Then Goldilocks tasted the porridge
in Baby Bear's bowl.

too   cold!   Then   Goldilocks   tasted

the   porridge   in   Baby   Bear's   bowl.

"Mmmmm – this is just right," she said.
And she ate it all up!

When she was finished,
Goldilocks went into the living room.

 all

 up!

 When

 she

 was

 finished,

Goldilocks went into the living room.

She sat in the great big chair,
but it was too high!

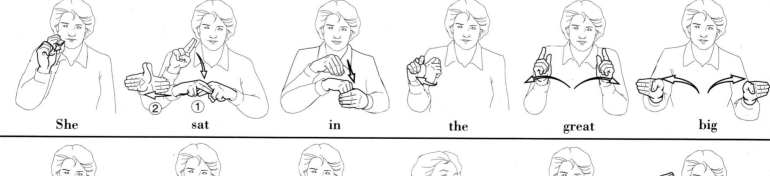

She   sat   in   the   great   big

chair,   but   it   was   too   high!

Next | she | sat | in | the | middle-

sized | chair, | but | it | was | too | low!

Next she sat in the middle-sized
chair, but it was too low!

Then Goldilocks sat in the wee little chair.
"This is just right!"

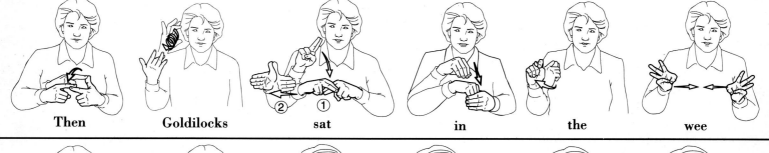

Then   Goldilocks   sat   in   the   wee

little   chair.   "This   is   just   right!"

She rocked back and forth. Suddenly, CRASH! The little chair broke to pieces!

She rocked back and forth.
Suddenly, CRASH!
The little chair broke to pieces!

Goldilocks felt tired,
so she went upstairs.

Goldilocks   felt   tired,   so   she   went   upstairs.

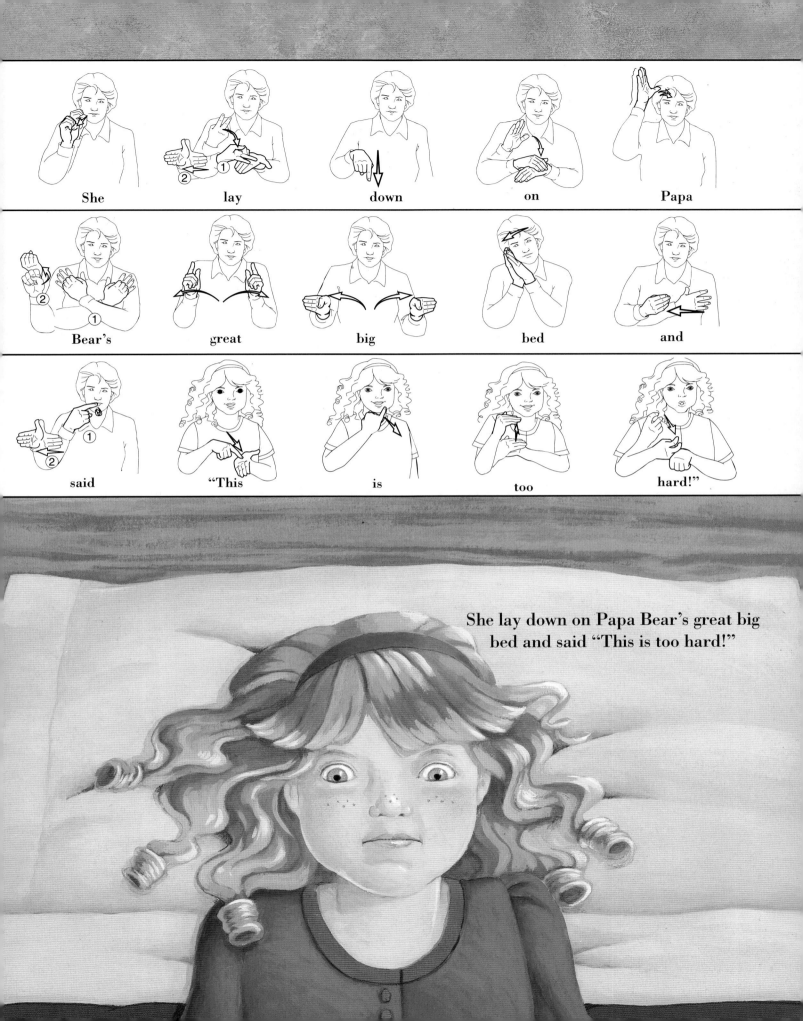

She	lay	down	on	Papa
Bear's	great	big	bed	and
said	"This	is	too	hard!"

She lay down on Papa Bear's great big bed and said "This is too hard!"

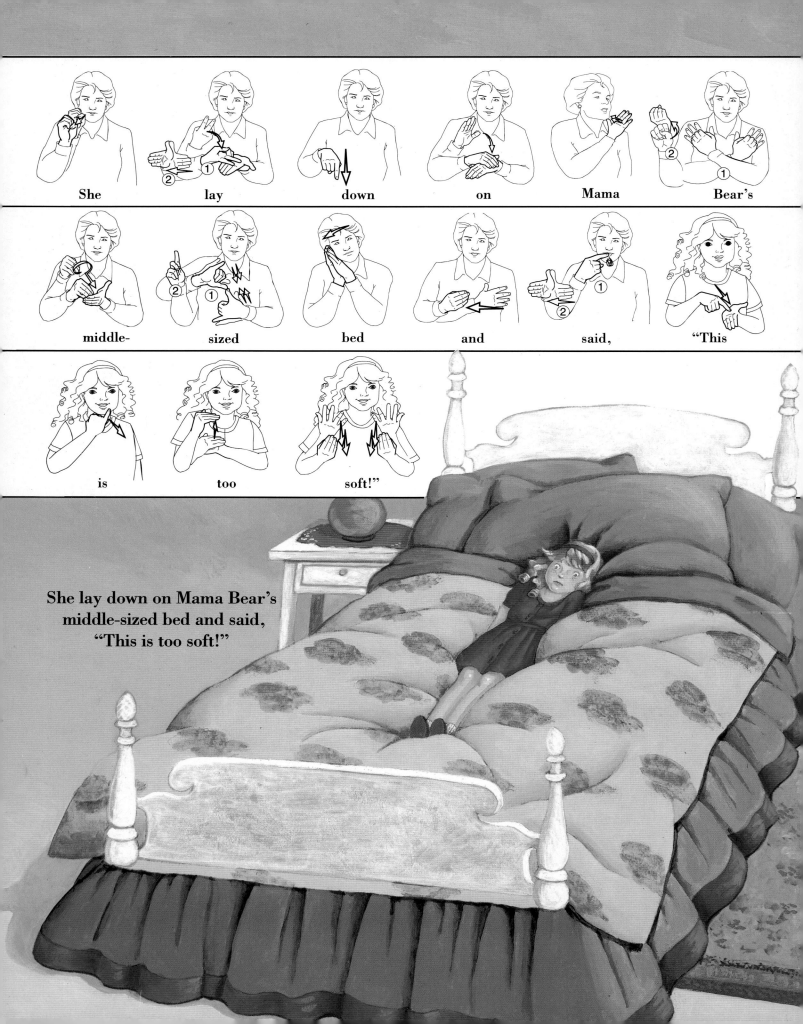

She lay down on Mama Bear's
middle-sized bed and said,
"This is too soft!"

Then she tried
Baby Bear's wee little bed.
"This is just right!" she said
and fell fast asleep!

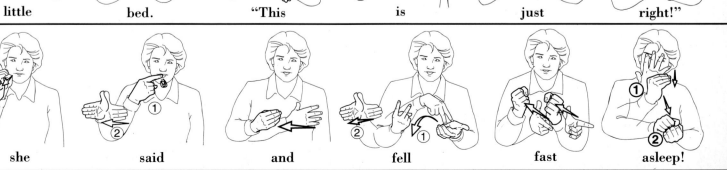

Then	she	tried	Baby	Bear's	wee
little	bed.	"This	is	just	right!"
she	said	and	fell	fast	asleep!

(cubs)

Soon, the three bears came home and went to the table.

Papa Bear said in
a great big voice,
"SOMEONE HAS BEEN
EATING MY PORRIDGE!"

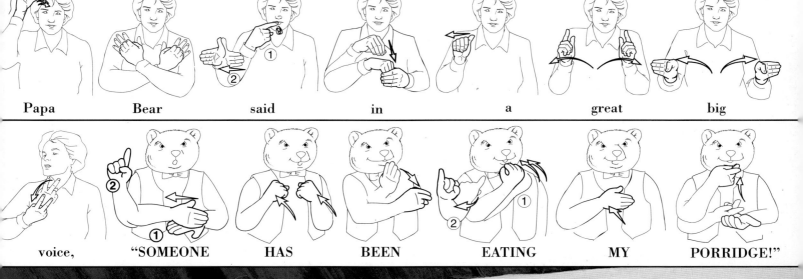

Papa	Bear	said	in	a	great	big

voice,	"SOMEONE	HAS	BEEN	EATING	MY	PORRIDGE!"

Mama Bear said in a middle-sized voice, "Someone has been eating my porridge."

"Someone has been eating
my porridge," cried Baby Bear
in a wee little voice,
"and it is ALL GONE!"

 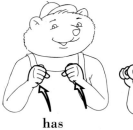 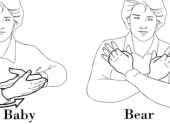     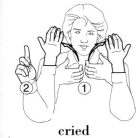 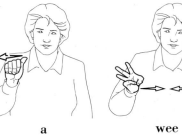

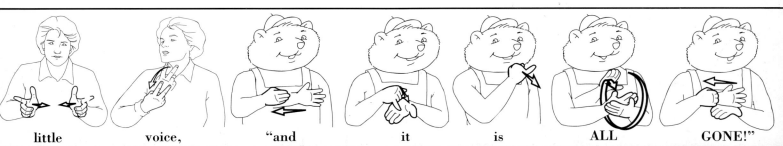

"Someone	has	been	eating	my	porridge,"
cried	Baby	Bear	in	a	wee
little	voice,	"and	it	is	ALL	GONE!"

Next, the three bears
went into the living room.
"SOMEONE HAS BEEN SITTING
IN MY CHAIR!"
said Papa Bear in a great big voice.

								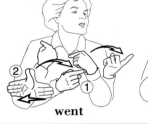		
Next,		the		three		bears		went		into

the	living	room.	"SOMEONE	HAS	BEEN

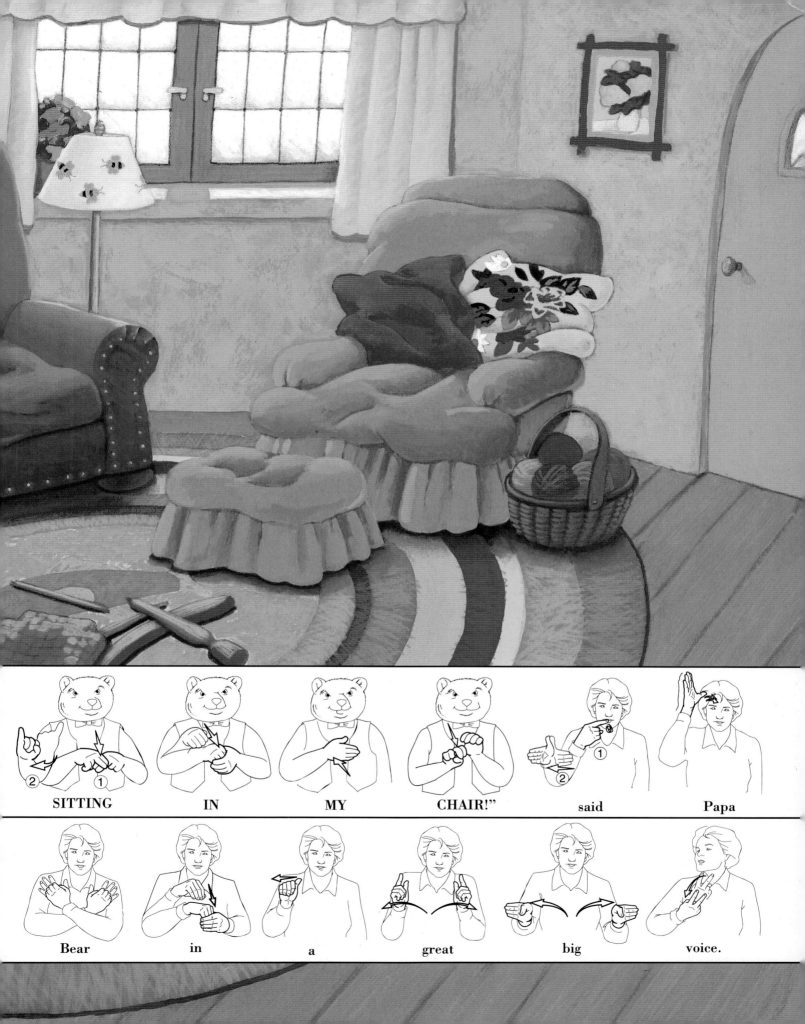

SITTING   IN   MY   CHAIR!"   said   Papa

Bear   in   a   great   big   voice.

"Someone	has	been	sitting	in

my	chair,"	said	Mama	Bear	in

a	middle-	sized	voice.

"Someone has been sitting in *my* chair,"
said Mama Bear in a middle-sized voice.

"Someone has been sitting in my chair,"
cried Baby Bear in a wee little voice,
"and BROKE IT TO PIECES!"

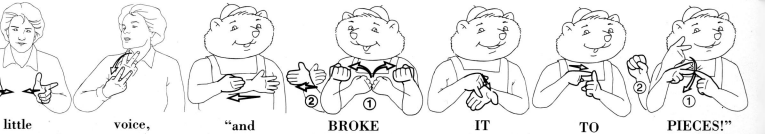

"Someone   has   been   sitting   in   my

chair,"   cried   Baby   Bear   in   a   wee

little   voice,   "and   BROKE   IT   TO   PIECES!"

| The | three | bears | went | upstairs | to | investigate. |

The three bears went upstairs to investigate.

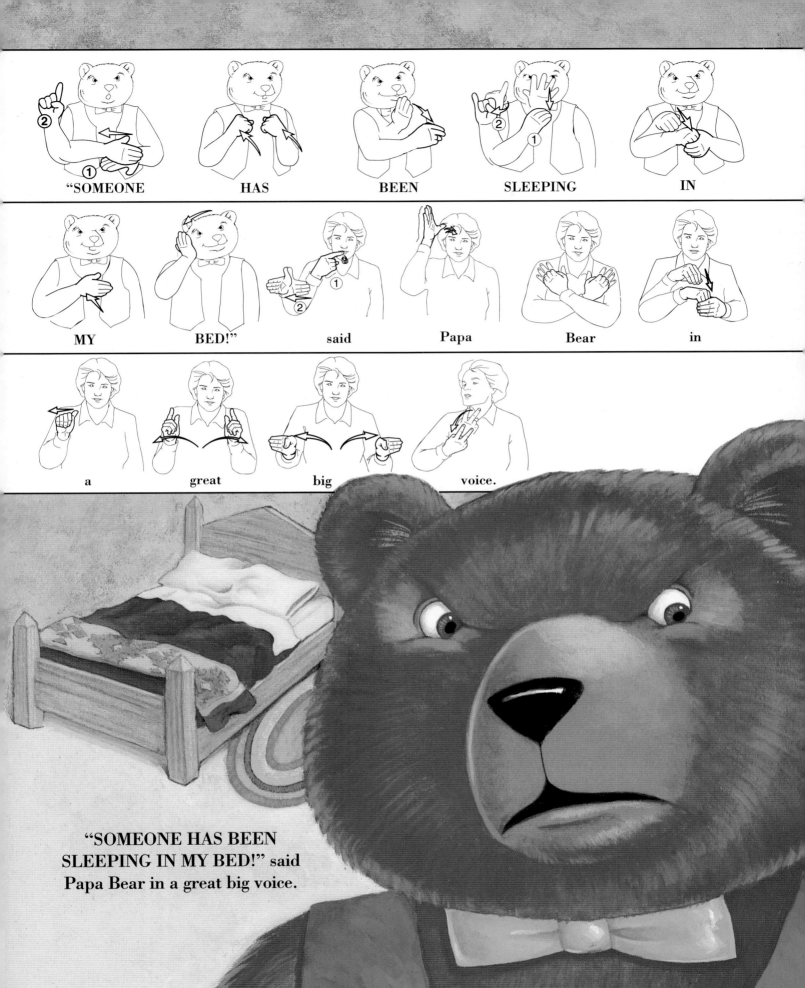

"SOMEONE   HAS   BEEN   SLEEPING   IN

MY   BED!"   said   Papa   Bear   in

a   great   big   voice.

"SOMEONE HAS BEEN
SLEEPING IN MY BED!" said
Papa Bear in a great big voice.

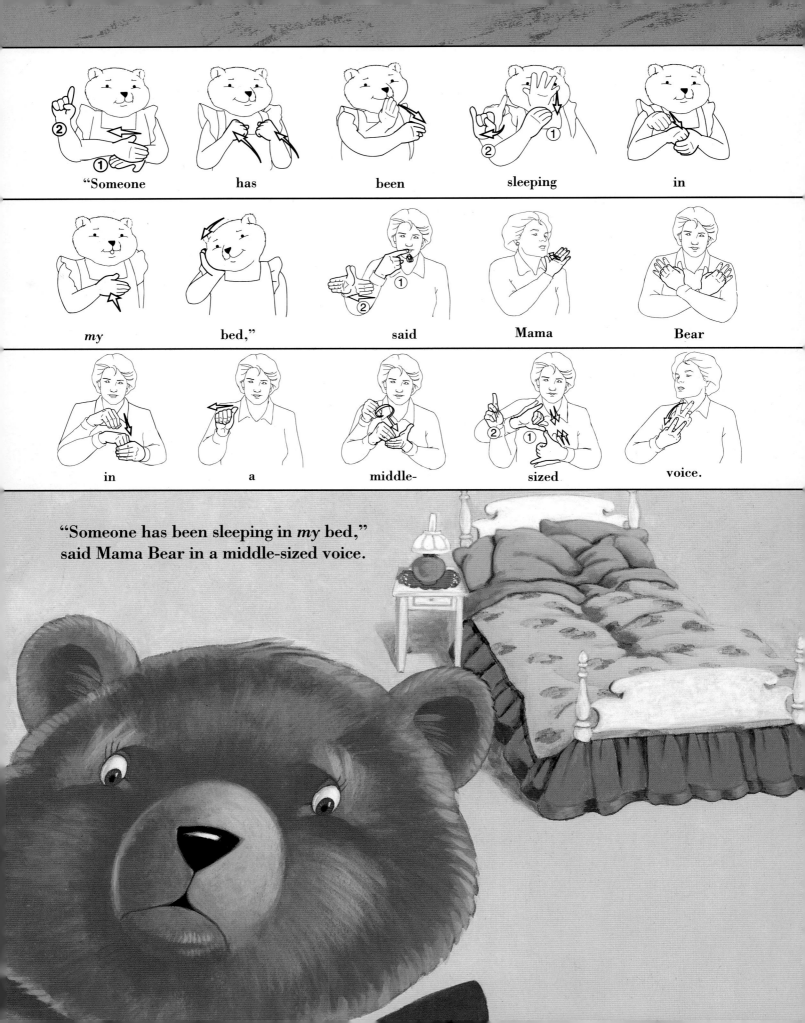

"Someone	has	been	sleeping	in
my	bed,"	said	Mama	Bear
in	a	middle-	sized	voice.

"Someone has been sleeping in *my* bed,"
said Mama Bear in a middle-sized voice.

"Someone	has	been	sleeping	in	my
bed,"	cried	Baby	Bear	in	a	wee
little	voice,	"and	THERE	SHE	IS!"

"Someone has been sleeping in my bed,"
cried Baby Bear in a wee little voice,
"and THERE SHE IS!"

Goldilocks woke up and saw the three bears.
"Oh, my!" she cried. She was frightened!

Goldilocks	woke	up	and	saw

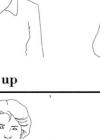

the	three	bears.	"Oh,	my!"

she   cried.   She   was   frightened.

She jumped out the window
and ran all the way home.
And the three bears never saw her again.

   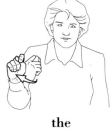  

She	jumped	out	the	window	and

ran	all	the	way	home.	And

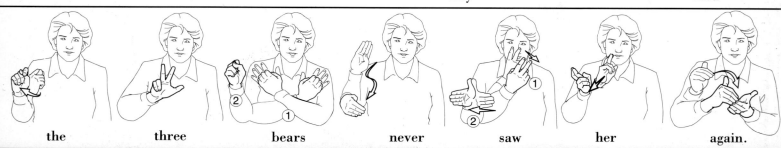

the	three	bears	never	saw	her	again.